SUNNING SEA LIONS: DISCOVERING EVEN NUMBERS

by Amanda Doering Tourville

illustrated by Sharon Holm

Content Consultant: Paula J. Maida, PhD, and Terry Sinko, Instructional Support Teacher

magic
Wagon

Text by Amanda Doering Tourville
Illustrations by Sharon Holm
Edited by Patricia Stockland
Interior layout and design by Becky Daum
Cover design by Becky Daum

Library of Congress Cataloging-in-Publication Data

Tourville, Amanda Doering, 1980–
  Sunning sea lions : discovering even numbers / by Amanda Doering Tourville ; illustrated by Sharon Holm.
     p. cm. — (Count the critters)
  ISBN 978-1-60270-267-7
  1. Counting—Juvenile literature. 2. Numbers, Natural—Juvenile literature. 3. Sea lions—Juvenile literature. I. Holm, Sharon Lane, ill. II. Title.
  QA113.T688 2009
  513.2'11—dc22

                    2008001616

Even numbers can be divided into groups of twos. See what even numbers look like as you learn about noisy California sea lions.

A colony of sea lions hauls out on the beach. Two male sea lions bark at each other to claim their spots. Two is an even number.

A colony of sea lions hauls out on the beach. Four sea lions quickly divide into groups of twos and swim to shore to escape a shark. Four is an even number.

A colony of sea lions hauls out on the beach. Six frisky pups chase each other in groups of twos. Six is an even number.

12 13 14 15 16 17 18 19 20

A colony of sea lions hauls out on the beach. Eight mother sea lions break into groups of twos to call to their pups. Eight is an even number.

12   13   14   15   16   17   18   19   20

A colony of sea lions hauls out on the beach. Ten mother sea lions rest in groups of twos to nurse their pups. Ten is an even number.

A colony of sea lions hauls out on the beach. Twelve sea lions divide into groups of twos and raise a flipper to cool off. Twelve is an even number.

A colony of sea lions hauls out on the beach. Fourteen sea lions waddle back to the ocean in groups of twos for a swim. Fourteen is an even number.

A colony of sea lions hauls out on the beach. Sixteen sea lions stretch out in the sun in groups of twos. Sixteen is an even number.

1 2 3 4 5 6 7 8 9 10 11

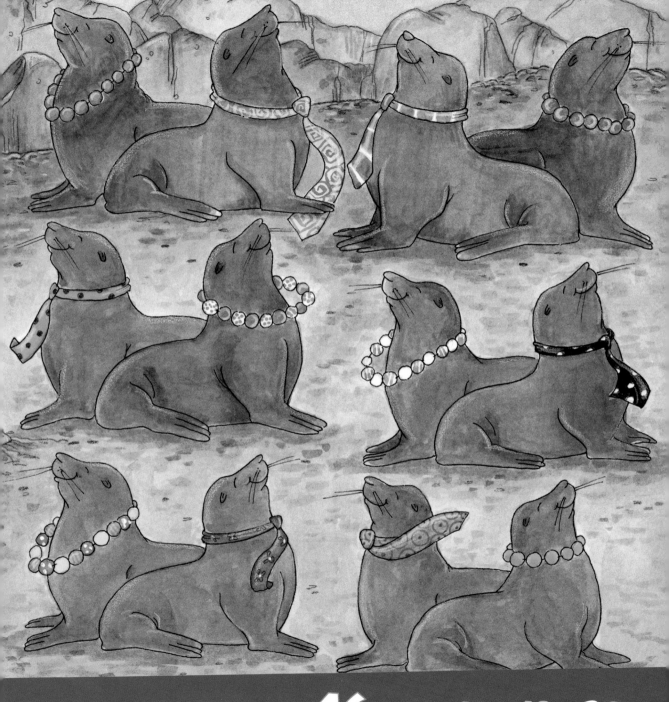

A colony of sea lions hauls out on the beach. Eighteen sea lions return to the water in groups of twos to hunt fish and squid. Eighteen is an even number.

A colony of sea lions hauls out on the beach. Twenty sea lions divide into groups of twos to snooze with their flippers tucked under their bodies. Twenty is an even number.

Words to Know

flipper—a sea lion's hands; sea lions use flippers to help them swim.

frisky—playful.

haul out—to leave the water for land.

waddle—to walk with short steps, moving from side to side.

Web Sites

To learn more about even numbers, visit ABDO Publishing Company on the World Wide Web at **www.abdopublishing.com**. Web sites about counting are featured on our Book Links page. These links are routinely monitored and updated to provide the most current information available.

1 2 3 4 5 6 7 8 9 10 11 12 13 14 15 16 17 18 19 20